Bear's Surprise Party

story by Joan Bowden
pictures by Jerry Scott

 GOLDEN PRESS
Western Publishing Company, Inc.
Racine, Wisconsin

To Sandy, Andrew, and Pamela Jane

Every night before she went to bed,
Bear made a wish.
Soon it would be her birthday.
And, more than anything,
Bear wanted a surprise party.
So she told her wish to her friends.

"Someone you know is having a birthday," Bear said. "A surprise party would be fun."

But Frog told Rabbit,
"It's not my birthday."

And Lamb told Duck,
"My birthday isn't until next spring."

"Besides, no one is *ever* surprised
at a surprise party,"
said Hen, Turtle, Squirrel, and Dog.
Then they forgot all about it.

But did that Bear give up?
She did not! "I know!" she said.
"I will give the birthday
party myself."

She sent a letter
to each of her friends.
It said:

Please come
to my house
on Saturday,
at half past
two.
It will be
a surprise!
Bear

But Frog told Rabbit,
"On Saturday we have to go fishing."

And Lamb told Duck,
"On Saturday we have to go shopping."

"Besides, Saturday is a very busy day,"
said Hen, Turtle, Squirrel, and Dog.
Then they thought no more about it.

So on Saturday, at half past two—
oh, what a *bad* surprise! No one came
to Bear's birthday party.

Then did she give up?
Oh, yes, she did! She felt so sad.
She sat right down and cried.
Sniff! Sniff! Sniff!

Outside, Frog heard
the *sniff, sniff, sniff*.
"Are you crying, Bear?"
he called.

The little bear
didn't want
to talk to anyone.
She called back,
"Go away, Frog!
I have a cold
in my head!"

But Frog didn't hear the words right.
He told Rabbit, "Guess what!
Bear has found *gold* on her head!
Tell the others!"

And Rabbit asked Lamb,
"Did you hear the news?
Bear has a *pole* on her head!
Tell the others!"

And Lamb told Duck, "Get help fast!
Bear has a *hole* in her head!
Tell the others!"

"Oh, wow!" cried Duck.
She was very surprised. She told Hen.

Then Hen called to Turtle,
"Help, Turtle, help!
Bear's in her house
with a *bowl*
on her head!
Tell the others!"

And Turtle told Squirrel,
"Do something fast!
Bear's in her house
with a *boat* in her *bed!*
Tell the *mothers!*"

And Squirrel called to Dog,
"Help, help, help!
Bear's *mouse* has a *goat*
on her *bread!* Tell your *brothers!*"

"Oh, bowwow *wow!*" barked Dog.
He was *very* surprised.

Then each friend told the others.
They told mothers and brothers.
And all of them ran to Bear's house
just as fast as they could.

When they got there, they saw
paper hats and colored strings.
They saw a cake and birthday things.

"But where is the *gold*
on Bear's head?" asked Frog.

Then everyone talked at once.

"Where is the *pole* on Bear's head?"

"The *hole* in her head?"

"The *bowl* on her head?"

"The *boat* in her *bed*?"

"The *goat*
on the *bread*?"

Everyone laughed.
"We didn't hear the
words right," they said.

But it didn't matter.
They had such fun!
Bear had the most fun of all!

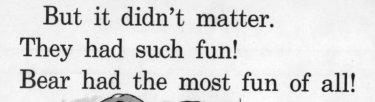

"All of us were surprised
at this surprise party," she said.
"How did it happen?"

"It's a very funny story," said Frog.
And it was!